D1294688

DAVY CROCKETT
FRONTIERSMAN

Retold by
ANDREW CODDINGTON

Illustrated by
MATÍAS LAPEGÜE

Cavendish
Square
New York

OVER TWO HUNDRED YEARS AGO, AMERICA WAS much different than it is today. In much of the country, there were no cities or roads, no police or hospitals. There were no grocery stores. People hunted animals and gathered wild plants for their dinners. There was no plumbing. People drank from streams and bathed under waterfalls. There was no electricity. Instead, people cooked over open fires and slept under the stars.

These parts were wild places. They were full of danger and adventure. These lands were called the frontier. Even though there were no laws or government, the frontier still had a king, and his name was Davy Crockett.

David "Davy" Crockett was born on August 17, 1786. He was the youngest of four brothers. The Crocketts lived in the woods of Tennessee, on the edge of the frontier. Davy's father, John, was an outdoorsman who fought in the American Revolution.

The Crocketts owned a tavern, a place where tired travelers could rest, get a meal, and share stories about their adventures. Young Davy heard many stories. Some talked about Native American tribes, attacks from bears and mountain lions, risky boat rides down raging river rapids, and mountains so tall they reached beyond the clouds. Soon, people would also tell stories about Davy.

It was not unusual back then for young boys to help their families by working. When Davy was twelve, his father sent him to work for a man named Jacob Siler. Siler steered cattle through the countryside. He needed help moving the cows across Virginia.

Davy was a strong boy and a good worker. Siler wanted Davy to keep working for him. When the job was over, he tried to kidnap Davy and make him work forever. Davy was too strong for Siler, though. Davy escaped, walking 7 miles (11 kilometers) to safety through knee-deep snow.

When Davy returned home safely, his parents sent him to school. But he didn't like spending his days in a crowded one-room schoolhouse. He dreamed of going on adventures.

Davy often skipped school. His father was not happy and often punished his son. Soon, Davy decided to run away.

Davy left one evening and did not come back for two years. He worked different jobs in different towns. Sometimes he fixed covered wagons that rumbled across the dirt roads of the frontier. Other times, he practiced his skills as a hunter and adventurer.

When Davy finally returned home at the age of sixteen, at first his family did not recognize him. He had grown to be taller than his three older brothers and even his father. Once they realized it was Davy, they welcomed him home with open arms.

As Davy grew older, he started dating. Eventually, he started seeing a girl named Mary Finley. Everyone called her Polly. Just before his twentieth birthday, Davy and Polly were married. They lived in the mountains of Tennessee for just over five years, and they had two sons, John Wesley and William.

Eventually, Davy wanted to live in the wilderness. Twice he moved his family farther into the western woods of Tennessee. He built a home along Rattlesnake Spring in Franklin County and called his new homestead "Kentuck."

Even as an adult, with a house, a wife, and a family, Davy Crockett still wished to go on adventures. In September 1813, just months after he built Kentuck, Davy joined the Tennessee militia. The militia was a group of citizens who joined together to protect their homes. Back then, American settlers in the frontier like Davy Crockett argued and fought with Native American tribes. Of course, the Native Americans just wanted to protect their homes, too.

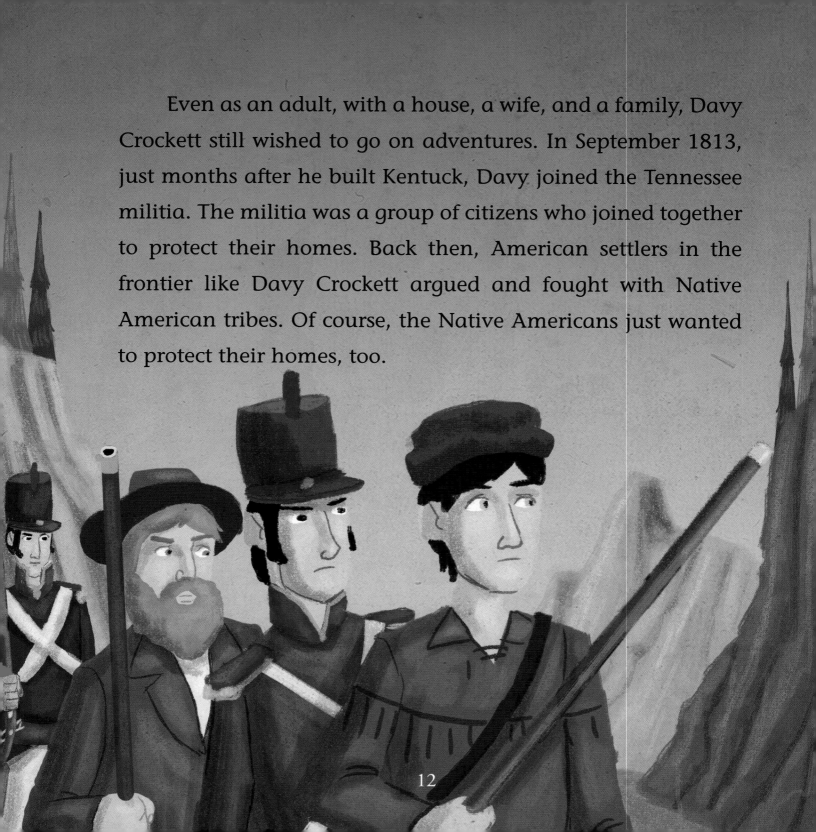

Davy Crockett's time in the militia took him all over the southern part of the United States. He fought in Alabama under a general named Andrew Jackson, who would one day become president. He marched through the swamps and muck of Florida, scouting for Native Americans.

Davy Crockett proved to be a great soldier. Growing up in the woods of Tennessee, he knew how to survive in the wild. He was a great hunter and an expert with his rifle, nicknamed "Betsy." He was also very smart.

Once, an army officer was surrounded by many Native Americans. He needed help, but Davy and another soldier were all who could come to his rescue. Davy knew that three against hundreds were not good odds, so he came up with a plan. He and the other soldier ran around the woods, making lots of noise and calling instructions to one another.

"Soldiers, move up!" they shouted. "Everyone, forward!"

The Native Americans grew frightened. It sounded like many soldiers were marching on them! They retreated back into the woods. Davy Crockett and the other soldier found the officer, who could not believe that only two men had come to his rescue. He thought the whole army was there for him!

Beyond battles with Native Americans, Davy Crockett had several brushes with danger. One of his favorite hobbies was bear hunting, but not all of his hunts went smoothly.

Once, when he was exploring Alabama, he became so sick that many said he had died. Imagine his family's surprise when he showed up at their door some time later, alive and well!

Another time, Davy was sailing down the Mississippi River when his boat wrecked. He nearly drowned in the river's muddy waters, but he swam against the strong waters and made it to shore.

When word of these stories got around, people across the United States started to call Davy Crockett the "Hero of the West" and the "King of the Frontier." They imagined him dressed in animal hides, with a gun slung over his shoulder and a coonskin cap for a crown. He became the subject of books, plays, and biographies, and his legend grew more and more incredible.

Along with serving on the militia, Davy Crockett also served in government. He served Tennessee in the state legislature and also represented his home state in Congress in Washington, DC.

Congressman Crockett wanted the United States to grow and more of the wilderness to be settled. He was a principled politician, but this got him into trouble. President Andrew Jackson suggested a law that would force Native Americans from their homes to make room for American settlers. Most people in Tennessee supported it, but Davy thought it was not fair to the Native Americans. They had lived there long before the settlers. He said he would not support the law, and this caused him to lose his seat in Congress.

Davy Crockett was unhappy with the deal-making in Washington and the behavior of the people of Tennessee. He yearned for the simple life in the wilderness, where a man could find adventure and freedom. So he did what he always did when he was unhappy: he moved west. In the 1830s, he packed up his home and family and moved to Texas.

Back then, Texas was part of Mexico. The Mexicans welcomed Americans to settle Texas in order to grow their own country. But the people of Texas soon wanted freedom and independence for themselves, and they fought with the Mexicans. Naturally, Davy Crockett joined the fight, too.

Davy Crockett joined Colonel William B. Travis and about two hundred other Texans at the Alamo, a Spanish mission that they had made into a fort. The Mexicans sent thousands of troops under General Antonio López de Santa Anna to remove the Texans. Although there were many more Mexicans than Texans, the Texans said they would not retreat.

The Texans held off the Mexicans for thirteen days, thanks in large part to Davy Crockett. Colonel Travis noted in his journal that Davy could be seen at all corners of the fort, encouraging the men to be brave. Davy also fought hard, taking a spot on the top of the Alamo's walls. Legend says that when he ran out of bullets and powder for his trusty rifle, he continued to fight anyway. He leapt into the trouble, swinging his gun like a club at any enemy soldier who charged him.

Eventually, the Mexicans proved too many for the Texans to hold off. The Mexicans swarmed the fort. Not many people know what happened to Davy Crockett. Some say he was captured by Santa Anna's troops and forced to work in a salt mine, but most people believe he died fighting at the Alamo.

When Colonel Travis's slave went searching for survivors, he said he found Crockett's body surrounded by dozens of Mexican soldiers. Although the King of the Frontier was dead, he never gave up the fight.

Today, the Alamo and Davy Crockett have become symbols of bravery, freedom, and strength. Davy Crockett lived up to his motto: "Be always sure you're right—then go a-head!"

ABOUT DAVY CROCKETT

David Crockett, known to popular history as "Davy," was an American frontiersman and statesman from Tennessee. Despite being the stuff of countless legends, some more farfetched than others, he accomplished much during his lifetime.

Growing up as the youngest of four sons of John Crockett in rural Tennessee, Davy Crockett grew up at the border of the United States and the western wilderness, a fact that came to shape his later ambitions. After spending his adolescence as a laborer, he joined the Tennessee militia and fought in the Creek Wars. His record as a military hero gained him popularity, and he occupied several offices during his political career, including Tennessee's congressional representative.

After being ousted from office for his opinions against the Indian Removal Act, he traveled to Texas, where he was instrumental in setting the goals of the local independence movement. It is thanks to Davy Crockett that Texas would become a republic. Crockett fought at the Alamo, where he likely died.

WORDS TO KNOW

frontier The lands beyond settled land, especially the western territories of the early United States.

homestead A house, especially a farm built by settlers.

legislature The part of government that makes laws.

militia A military force made up of ordinary citizens.

mission A church building built by Christians to convert local people.

principled Acting with morals or knowing the difference between right and wrong.

TO FIND OUT MORE

BOOKS

Crockett, David. *Davy Crockett: His Own Story: Narrative of the Life of David Crockett.* Bedford, MA: Applewood Books, 1993.

Herman, Gail. *Who Was Davy Crockett?* New York: Penguin Group, 2013.

Krensky, Stephen. *Davy Crockett: A Life on the Frontier.* New York: Simon Spotlight, 2004.

WEBSITES

The Alamo

http://www.history.com/topics/alamo

The History Channel's website on the Alamo explores the history and impact of the battle of the Alamo.

In Search of David Crockett

http://www.tnhistoryforkids.org/insearchof/david_crockett

Tennessee History for Kids offers this collection of ten facts about David Crockett.

ABOUT THE AUTHOR

Andrew Coddington has written numerous books for Cavendish Square on topics including myths and legends, paranormal creatures, and world history. He lives in Lancaster, New York, with his wife and dog. He enjoys exploring the outdoors like Davy Crockett (but he thinks it's important to stay in school!).

ABOUT THE ILLUSTRATOR

Matías Lapegüe was born in Buenos Aires, Argentina, in 1977. As a child, he enjoyed drawing animations from science fiction movies. As a teenager, he dedicated his time to sports. Later on he fell in love again with drawing. He graduated with a degree in graphic design in 2004 and worked as a freelancer both in graphic and web design. Lapegüe studied digital color with Nestor Pereyra, a well-respected colorist. He is currently creating new worlds and characters for young and old alike.

Published in 2017 by Cavendish Square Publishing, LLC
243 5th Avenue, Suite 136, New York, NY 10016

Copyright © 2017 by Cavendish Square Publishing, LLC

First Edition

No part of this publication may be reproduced, stored in a retrieval system, or transmitted in any form or by any means—electronic, mechanical, photocopying, recording, or otherwise—without the prior permission of the copyright owner. Request for permission should be addressed to Permissions, Cavendish Square Publishing, 243 5th Avenue, Suite 136, New York, NY 10016. Tel (877) 980-4450; fax (877) 980-4454.

Website: cavendishsq.com

This publication represents the opinions and views of the author based on his or her personal experience, knowledge, and research. The information in this book serves as a general guide only. The author and publisher have used their best efforts in preparing this book and disclaim liability rising directly or indirectly from the use and application of this book.

CPSIA Compliance Information: Batch #CW17CSQ

All websites were available and accurate when this book was sent to press.

Cataloging-in-Publication Data

Names: Coddington, Andrew.
Title: Davy Crockett: frontiersman / Andrew Coddington.
Description: New York : Cavendish Square Publishing, 2017. | Series: American legends and folktales | Includes index.
Identifiers: ISBN 9781502622679 (pbk.) | ISBN 9781502621931 (library bound) | ISBN 9781502621924 (6 pack) | ISBN 9781502621948 (ebook)
Subjects: LCSH: Crockett, Davy, 1786-1836--Juvenile fiction. | Pioneers--Tennessee--Biography--Juvenile fiction.
Classification: LCC PZ7.C633 Dav 2017 | DDC [F] --dc23

Editorial Director: David McNamara
Editor: Kristen Susienka
Copy Editor: Nathan Heidelberger
Associate Art Director: Amy Greenan
Designer: Alan Sliwinski
Illustrator: Matías Lapegüe
Production Coordinator: Karol Szymczuk

Printed in the United States of America